the five senses

hearing

María Rius

J.M. Parramón   J.J. Puig

BARRON'S

Woodbury, New York • London • Toronto • Sydney

Listen! Can you hear that sound?

Listen to the bells ringing.

Listen to the children singing...

...and the sound of music...

...and the song of the birds...

...and the whistling of the train.

Hello! Can you hear me?

Yes! I hear you!

Can you hear that noise?
It's the sound of the waves.

Can you hear this noise?
It's dogs barking!

Wheeeoooo! Listen to your echo!

Yelling sounds terrible!

A nice low voice sounds much, much better.

Now, listen carefully!

Everything that you hear, you hear
with your EARS.

HEARING

This is the way your *ears* work. Your ears act almost like telephones that send sound messages to your brain.

When something makes a noise, or when someone talks, the air begins to vibrate, or move, in waves. These are called *sound waves.* If the sound is high, the sound waves are short. If the sound is low, the sound waves are long. These sound waves travel through the air until they reach your *outer ear.*

Once the waves start moving down your *ear canal,* all kinds of things begin moving. First the sound waves strike the *eardrum,* which starts to vibrate. These vibrations jiggle the *hammer,* which then jiggles the *anvil,* which then jiggles the *stirrup.* The hammer, the anvil, and the stirrup are tiny little bones in your *middle ear.*

The stirrup then starts the *cochlea* jiggling. The *cochlea* is just like a shell (the name means "cockle shell") that's filled with liquid. The liquid starts jiggling, and that causes tiny hairs lining the cochlea to start jiggling, too. These hairs then send a message along the *auditory nerve* right to your brain.

Once your brain gets the sound message, it does its best to figure out what the sound means, and what you should do about it. If you were a little mouse running across the floor and you heard the meow of a cat, your brain would figure it out. Then your brain would tell you what to do. *Run!*

Your ear does one other thing. It helps you keep your balance. The part of your *inner ear* called the *semicircular canals* lets you know whether you are sitting, or standing, or lying down. If you spin around for too long, you can get your poor *semicircular canals* all confused—and that's called being dizzy.